7/3

Pu 1978

W9-CKC-374

612.3

CYA/BSC 5/78

AWARD(S) WON

Notable Children's Books   1978

ABOUT THE BOOK

William Beaumont had grown up with the idea that he would be famous. But as the army surgeon at a fort in the wilderness of Mackinac Island, Michigan Territory, he felt that life was passing him by.

Then, on June 6, 1822, there was a shooting accident in the village near the fort that would radically alter the course of Beaumont's life. Alexis St. Martin, a hardy frontiersman in the fur trade, had been shot, leaving a hole in his stomach that would never close up, even after Dr. Beaumont had healed him. Through that hole, a clear passageway into the stomach from outside the body, the doctor decided to perform experiments on digestion, which had been a mystery to science for centuries. If his experiments succeeded, he would win the kind of fame he'd dreamed of.

How William Beaumont won an enduring place in history through his remarkable discoveries on digestion is the basis of this fascinating story.

DR. BEAUMONT

AND THE MAN WITH
THE HOLE IN HIS STOMACH

by Sam and Beryl Epstein
illustrated by Joseph Scrofani

COWARD, McCANN & GEOGHEGAN, INC
NEW YORK

ISBN 0-698-30680-5 lib. bdg.

Library of Congress Cataloging in Publication Data
Epstein, Samuel.   Dr. Beaumont and the man with the hole in his stomach.
(A Science Discovery book)
SUMMARY: A biography of a curious physician and the unusual patient who enabled him to carry out experiments concerning digestion.
1. Digestion—Juvenile literature. 2. Beaumont, William, 1785-1853—Juvenile literature. 3. United States. Army—Surgeons—Biography—Juvenile literature. 4. St. Martin, Alexis, 1797?-1880—Juvenile literature. 5. Fur trades—Canada—Biography—Juvenile literature. [1. Beaumont, William, 1785-1853, 2. St. Martin, Alexis, 1797?-1880. 3. Physicians. 4. Digestion] I. Epstein, Beryl Williams, 1910-   joint author. II. Scrofani, Joseph. III. Title.
QP145.E67   612′.3 [920]   77-8236

For Mary Squire Abbot,
with gratitude and love
—*S. & B. E.*

To Kathy, for all her patience
—*J. S.*

CONTENTS

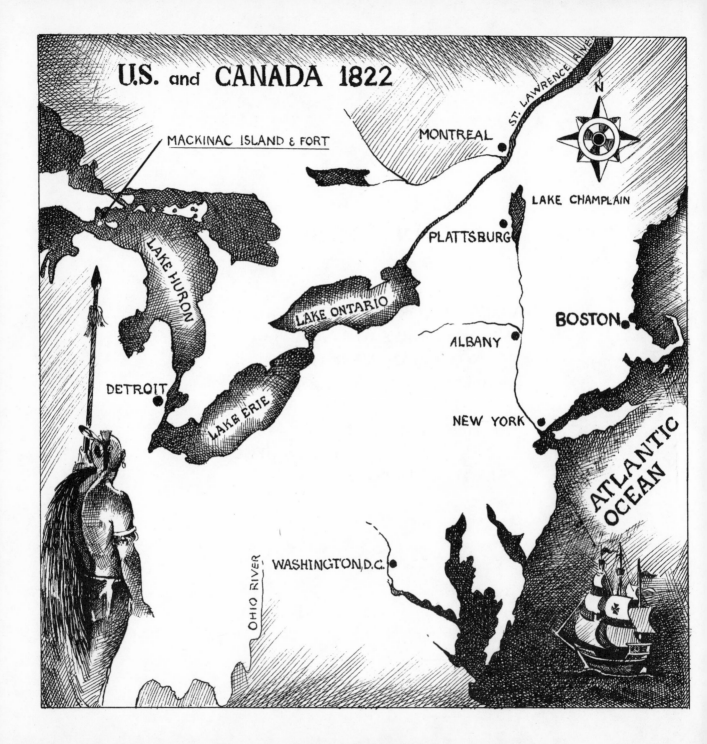

1 / THE ARMY DOCTOR AND THE VOYAGEUR

The strange-but-true story of Dr. William Beaumont and Alexis St. Martin, "the man with the hole in his stomach," began on Mackinac Island on June 6, 1822. That green little island is in Lake Huron, near the shore of what is now Michigan. It was known then as the Michigan Territory.

Most of the Territory was a forest wilderness inhabited by the Hurons, the Chippewas, the Ottawas and other Indian tribes. But on Mackinac Island there was a fort manned by a company of the United States Army, and a tiny village that had grown up around the American Fur Company's headquarters and store.

In that store Dr. Beaumont and Alexis St. Martin had their first fateful encounter. Only an accident could have brought them together. They were so different in every way that, if they'd had their choice, they would never have spent a moment in each other's company.

William Beaumont's father was a prosperous Connecticut farmer, but William hadn't been interested in farming. Farmers seldom became famous, he thought. And, as he'd grown up, the idea that he would become a famous man grew with him.

After trying schoolteaching and clerking in a store, he decided on a career in medicine. He got his training, as most medical students did then, by apprenticing himself to a doctor. He was about to set up in practice for himself when the War of 1812 broke out. He immediately joined the army's medical corps.

On the battlefields of that war he found some of the glory and excitement he'd been looking for. He was "wading in blood, cutting off arms, legs . . . " he boasted in his diary. "I cut and slashed for forty-eight hours without food or sleep," he added. And he was awarded a citation for bravery.

But the glory and excitement ended when the war was over and he found himself a small-town doctor in Plattsburgh, New York.

"I'm trapped," he growled angrily to Deborah Green, the gentle-voiced Quaker widow who served the guests at her father's inn. "Trapped among colicky babies and old ladies with lumbago!"

"But thee is a good doctor," she told him. "And surely it should satisfy any man to know that he can help those who are sick or hurt."

But it didn't satisfy Dr. William Beaumont. He was in his

thirties by then, and he felt that his chances for fame were slipping away.

One day he received a letter from Dr. Joseph Lovell, a wartime friend who'd become Surgeon General of the Army. Dr. Lovell asked if Dr. Beaumont wanted to serve another term as an army surgeon.

Dr. Beaumont answered that he did indeed, provided he were given a frontier post. Out in the Territories, where Indian uprisings still took place, a man could become a hero overnight!

Some weeks later Dr. Beaumont was standing at the rail of the new vessel, *Walk-on-the-Water,* the first steamboat on Lake Huron. Mackinac Island was just up ahead. Soon he could make out the thick limestone walls of the fort crowning the hill above the little harbor. Three sturdy blockhouses, spaced along the walls, protected the long ramp leading up the hillside to the fort's south sally port, or entrance. Would attacking Indians try to use that ramp? the doctor wondered.

Suddenly the sound of hideous war whoops reached him across the water. Flames leaped up from the beach beside the harbor. There was the flash and noise of gunfire.

"An attack!" Dr. Beaumont turned away from the rail, eager to alert the others on board. "The island is being attacked!"

A member of the ship's crew, standing nearby, stared at him for a moment and then burst into laughter.

"That's nothing but the *voyageurs* and the Indians from hereabouts," he said when he could speak. "The Indians come

11 /

to the American Fur Company with their furs every June. And the voyageurs arrive at the same time with the furs they've collected from the Indians to the north and the west. So they all spend their money on liquor at the company store, and enjoy themselves together."

Dr. Beaumont was furious. He hated being laughed at. And he felt cheated to learn that Mackinac Island, surrounded by friendly Indians, wasn't the kind of dangerous post he'd expected. He turned his back on the crewman and stalked off, muttering that Indians and their voyageur friends seemed more like animals than men. It was an opinion he never changed.

There was little about Mackinac Island that he did find to like, except for Robert Stuart, the Fur Company manager, and his elegant wife. Most of the fort's officers bored him. The enlisted men were beneath his notice. And he didn't have enough work to keep him busy.

Before a year was out he had returned to Plattsburgh on a brief leave, and brought Deborah Green back to the island as his bride.

Deborah was a great success in the tiny community. She and the elegant Mrs. Stuart planned dinner parties and evenings when Deborah read aloud in her gentle voice. "They help pass the time," she told her husband cheerfully.

"Yes, they do that," Dr. Beaumont glumly agreed. But he couldn't forget that while he was passing time, other men somewhere out in the world were winning the kind of fame he felt should be his.

· · ·

As for Alexis St. Martin, the idea of becoming famous had never entered his head. He'd been born to poor parents in a small village not far from Montreal. He'd never learned to read or write. All he knew of the world outside his village were stories of Paris, the beautiful city French-Canadians thought of as the center of the world. When the American Fur Company's hiring agent arrived, during his regular tour of eastern Canada, Alexis joined the other able-bodied young men who crowded around him. They all hoped for jobs as voyageurs.

Stocky dark-haired Alexis was one of those hired. He was strong and fit. The work suited him perfectly. All winter his home was a heavy canoe called a bateau. He and the seven other voyageurs who made up its crew could paddle tirelessly for hours, even against a strong current. They could pick up the bateau and its steadily growing load of furs and carry the whole weight overland from one body of water to the next.

The clerk who traveled with them directed their journey from one Indian village to another. Sometimes, while he bartered for a village's hoard of furs, the voyageurs were handsomely entertained by friendly Indian hosts. But often, when the villages were far apart, they had little to eat and slept in the open, sheltered only by their overturned canoe.

As the long winter season came to an end, they could look forward to a glorious summer. They put ashore for one last time, as they neared Mackinac Island, and decorated their bateau with flowering branches. Then they headed straight for the island.

Several other bateaux would be entering Mackinac harbor along with theirs. The race among them began instantly. Faster and faster all the voyageurs thrust their paddles into the water. Faster and faster all the heavy bateaux streaked forward until it seemed they would all pile up on the beach in one great tangle of men and furs and splintered wood.

But at the last possible moment each paddle dug deep and held. The huge bateaux were slowed to a near halt. Then the prow of each one would slide gently up the sloping sand and come to rest.

Alexis would be shouting as loudly as all the rest as they leaped ashore after their skillful performance. The Indians would be waiting to welcome their friends with food and drink. Alexis would still be spluttering over his first fiery swallow from one of the liquor jugs when they started for the company store. They wouldn't consider the summer truly begun until they'd each bought one of the high black hats that was a voyageur's proud trademark.

That night there would be bragging tales of the winter's journeys, wild dancing around a blazing fire, and fights that were part wrestling matches and part slugging contests. Sometimes the winner of a fight won the right to wear a feather in his hat as a sign that he had become champion of his crew.

Alexis may have dreamed that someday he would be

wearing a feather in his own hat. But since he couldn't guess what was going to happen to him, he would have felt he had plenty of time for that. Long happy years as a voyageur seemed to stretch ahead of him.

• • •

On June 6, 1822, Alexis St. Martin was among the group of men loafing away an afternoon in the company store. A drunken voyageur, only a few feet away from Alexis, was showing off the gun he'd just bought. Perhaps there was a scuffle. Perhaps someone simply jostled the gun owner. But somehow, suddenly, it happened. The gun swung toward Alexis, and at that same moment it went off.

The full load of powder and buckshot tore into Alexis' body from the side, just below his breast.

As the smoke cleared, men backed silently away from the body lying on the floor. Small flames were flickering along the torn edges of Alexis' jacket, around a monstrously gaping wound. Then blood spurted from the wound and drowned the flames.

Robert Stuart spoke finally, his voice hoarse with shock.

"Fetch the doctor!" he ordered.

2 / A TERRIBLE WOUND

Dr. Beaumont strode briskly down the hill from the fort. He was in a hurry to treat this case, whatever it might prove to be, and return to Deborah. She was expecting their first child at any moment.

Robert Stuart himself awaited him in the doorway of the squat building on Market Street that housed the company store.

"In here, Beaumont," Stuart said, and led him into the storeroom with its rough counter and crowded shelves.

"We carried the poor fellow into the back room," Stuart went on, walking past a hushed crowd toward the rear of the store. He stepped around a large dark puddle on the floor, and the doctor saw that it was a pool of blood.

"We tried to remove his clothes," Stuart was saying. "But the jacket had been burned and the charred cloth had been—been driven in! The load of powder and buckshot struck him with terrible force, from only a few feet away." He stepped through the door at the back of the store. "Here he is."

Dr. Beaumont stared down at the dark-haired voyageur lying unconscious on a crude cot. Even during the fiercest battles of the war he had never seen a wound like this.

Part of the man's abdomen just below his left breast had been completely blown away. Blackened edges of cloth and skin, and ends of torn muscles and ligaments, surrounded a bloody cavity larger than a man's hand. The stench of burned flesh reached the doctor's nostrils.

Near the upper edge of the wound was a charred pinkish lump or protrusion as big as a turkey egg. It pulsed regularly, giving off a thick bloody fluid with each pulsation. It was, the doctor realized, part of the man's left lung, somehow thrust forward out of the rib cage!

Then he saw that there was also a second protrusion, almost as large and just below the first. There was a hole in it through which the doctor could have thrust his finger. Through that hole trickled what appeared to be bits of chewed meat and other foods.

Could it possibly be the man's stomach, pierced by buckshot? the doctor asked himself. No! he thought at first. No man could live even for an instant if his stomach were exposed like this, and punctured through all its layers. And this man was alive. He was still breathing.

Yet there was nothing else it could be. Dr. Beaumont knew that he was indeed looking at an exposed stomach. A stomach with a hole in it.

19 /

He was certain that the man could not survive for longer than a few minutes. Nevertheless his duty as a doctor was clear. He opened his bag and knelt beside the cot.

First, very gently, he pushed with his fingertips against that protruding pinkish lump. It didn't yield. It seemed to be caught on something. He slid a finger beneath it and touched a sharp point.

He knew it was bone he was feeling, the bone of a rib. But half of the rib had been broken off. Shot away, he assumed. And the lung's delicate membrane was caught on the pointed half remaining.

He reached for his penknife, lifted the lung with his left forefinger, and used the sharp blade to clip off that point.

Then once more his bloodied fingertips thrust gently against the protruding lung. This time he was able to push it back into the rib cage. And there, in full sight, it continued to pulse, giving off air and bloody mucus with each expiration. The doctor could feel the air, like a faint breath, against his hand.

Next he wiped away the food oozing from the stomach. He pressed the stomach back into the cavity of the abdomen. He removed those bits of cloth and other loose fragments that came away easily when he touched them. Then he laid a cloth dressing over the whole wound, pressing it firmly against the lung and the hole in the stomach. There was little more he could do, he thought.

"I will be back in an hour," he told Stuart as he closed his bag and rose to his feet.

21 /

But to himself he thought, That man will be dead before I am back in my quarters.

An hour later the man lay just as Dr. Beaumont had left him. He was still breathing. Therefore he had to be cared for as if he had a chance of recovery.

Removing the dressing, Dr. Beaumont probed deeply into the torn flesh. One by one he drew out shreds of gun wadding, buckshot, scraps of cloth, ragged bits of muscle and ligament, slivers of bone. It was a slow job.

Finally the wound was cleaned as thoroughly as possible. Now the doctor needed a different dressing from the simple one he had first applied.

He took for granted that the wound—if his patient remained alive long enough—would become what he called fetid. That is, it would develop pus and become feverish. Today that condition is described as infected, and is known to be caused by germs. But in 1822 no one knew that germs cause disease and infection. Dr. Beaumont therefore wouldn't attempt to cover the wound with an antiseptic dressing that would protect it from germs.

Instead he had in mind a dressing made with yeast. As the yeast fermented it would, he hoped, bring on the fetid condition very quickly. Pus and fever, he believed, were necessary parts of the healing process.

Mixing yeast with flour, charcoal and hot water, he formed a wet pad, or poultice, and laid it over the wound. It would have to be replaced as soon as the fermenting stopped—if the patient was still alive by then.

Before leaving the company store, the doctor asked Stuart for his patient's name. Stuart shrugged. Since the voyageurs themselves couldn't spell their names—couldn't write them either, of course—Stuart could only tell the doctor what it sounded like.

So the first note Dr. Beaumont made on his unusual new case began, "Alex Samata, St. Martin, San Maten, a Canadian lad about 19 years old, hardy, robust and healthy, was accidentally shot by the unlucky discharge of a gun on the 6th of June, 1822."

On the 8th of June, two days later, Deborah gave birth to a daughter they named Sarah. She was a healthy baby. Deborah felt very well herself. She was soon urging her husband to leave her long enough to visit the strange patient whose name they would eventually know to be Alexis St. Martin.

By then, with permission of the fort's commander, Alexis had been moved to the little hospital inside the fort. For the next several days he ran a high fever.

His symptoms, Dr. Beaumont wrote, were of "violent pneumonia and inflammation of the lungs." The doctor treated them, as was common at the time, by opening a vein and drawing out nearly a pint of blood. The bleeding, he noted, "gave relief." The wound, which had become "very fetid," he treated by daily cleaning and fresh poultices.

The month of June wore slowly away. Each morning Dr. Beaumont was amazed to find his patient still alive.

"It is a most remarkable case," he told Deborah.

"Thee has given him excellent care," she said.

Sometimes she visited Alexis herself. He was not really conscious, but she had seen his eyes flicker, his feet shift restlessly on the cot, when the sound of the voyageurs' singing came up from the beach.

By September the island had fallen quiet again. The voyageurs and the Indians had departed. Soon winter settled in. Little Sarah—her parents called her Tasey—was thriving.

Alexis was still too weak to get up, but he was slowly improving. The doctor ordered a healthy diet for him: "Arrowroot, Crackers, Robbins broiled or in soup."

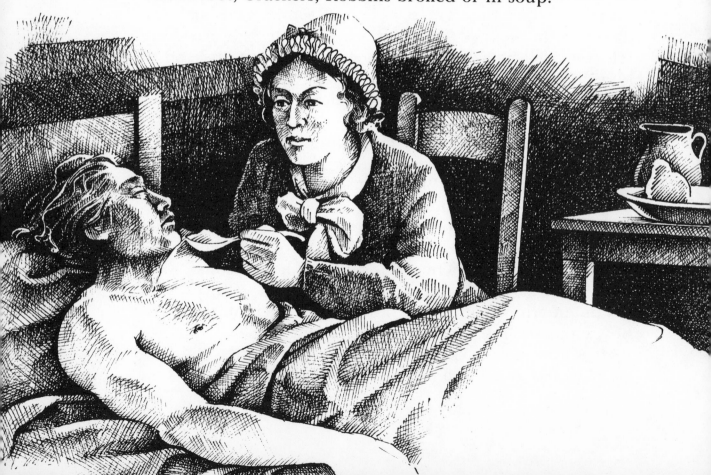

Everything Alexis ate, of course, trickled away through that hole in his stomach unless a dressing kept it inside. The best dressing, Dr. Beaumont finally decided, was a small plug of lint, pushed into the hole like a cork in a bottle and held in place with adhesive strips. Lint, a soft fuzzy substance made by scraping linen cloth, was the usual bandaging material of the time.

By the year's end Alexis' fever had long since disappeared. Scar tissue had formed around the edges of the wound and was spreading toward its center. The injured part of the lung had sloughed off—dried up and fallen away. It left the rest of the lung perfectly healthy.

Bits of the protruding stomach had also sloughed off. And the flesh near that hole had adhered, or stuck, to the muscles between the ribs. Scar tissue was forming over those muscles now too, but it formed around the hole in the stomach, not over it. So the hole remained, a clear passageway into the stomach from outside the body.

Eventually that hole looked rather like a mouth pursed up, ready to whistle. A loose flap of stomach lining often came down over it, closing it off, in the same way a tongue might close off the mouth's opening into the throat. But Dr. Beaumont could easily push that flap aside and look through the hole to see what he was sure no man had ever seen before—the interior of the stomach of a living man.

After a time, when he had looked at the wound day after day, Dr. Beaumont had an idea. An account of Alexis' injury and his recovery under a doctor's faithful care would make an interesting article for a medical journal. The more he thought about it, the more he liked the idea. The article would certainly win recognition for its author, even if the recognition came only from other doctors.

Dr. Beaumont suddenly felt more cheerful than he had in a long time. Now he took a new interest in making careful accurate notes on the progress of his highly interesting case.

In the spring the fort commander said that since Alexis St. Martin was not a soldier he must leave the fort hospital. The Fur Company refused to support Alexis, since he was no longer a useful company employee. Penniless and still helpless, the once-proud voyageur became an object of the town's charity.

The patient's room and board in the village cost the townspeople $10 a month. His "surgical aids and medicine" cost them an additional sum. By the time the townspeople had paid out $150 they decided they had done enough for a useless pauper.

"They are sending Alexis back to Canada—to Montreal!" Dr. Beaumont said, striding into Deborah's kitchen in a rage.

Deborah raised floury hands from the bread she was kneading. "But he could never survive traveling two thousand miles in an open boat!" she said.

"Of course he could not!" Dr. Beaumont snapped. "This town is truly the Kingdom of Satan!"

Deborah had often seen her husband angry, but seldom as angry as this. And she understood why. For one thing, of course, no doctor who had saved a life would want to see that life thrown away. But the more important thing, she knew, was that her husband wouldn't be able to write the article he'd been talking so much about. If Alexis were sent off before he was fully recovered, Dr. Beaumont couldn't fully record the cure. Deborah knew how much that article meant to her husband.

"We could keep Alexis here," she offered. "In our quarters."

"Here!" Dr. Beaumont stared at her. How could he take a lout of a voyageur into his own home?

Yet he had to admit Deborah's plan would give him time to complete the treatment of his case and write about his success. He hated to think that article might never be written.

Deborah saw his difficulty and helped him out. "I'm sure Alexis would wish to serve both thee and me in any way he could, as soon as he becomes able," she said.

"Ah yes! No doubt that is so," Dr. Beaumont said. His wife's words had put quite a different light on the matter. Alexis would be their servant!

"Very well," he said. "We shall bring him here."

The next day Alexis became part of the Beaumont household.

3 / NOT A MAN, A FREAK

At first Alexis' wound still needed daily dressing, and he could move about only slowly. But in time he was able to do light tasks. He could sweep the floor for Deborah and brush the doctor's uniform. And he was glad to work, to show his gratitude and because it kept him busy. Sometimes he could almost forget how lonely he was, shut away with people who would always be strangers to him.

By the next spring, two years after his "fatal" injury, Alexis St. Martin felt completely well. The plug of lint in his side hardly troubled him. He could run errands and chop wood. He was eager now to see his old friends and tell them that he was ready to join them again.

He was playing with little Tasey one June day when the first of the bateaux returned. He lifted her up to the window so they could both watch the dramatic race across the harbor. Soon the voyageurs would be buying their hats.

"Next year you will see Alexis on one of those bateaux," he told Tasey. "You will be very proud."

That night he slipped out of the doctor's quarters and hurried down the hill to the beach. One of the jugs of fiery liquor came into his hand almost as soon as he joined the noisy throng around the fires. He took one long swallow and then another. He might not have any bragging stories to tell, when the storytelling began, but he was sure he could still drink as well as any man on the island that night.

After the third drink he felt as if those long months under the doctor's care had never happened. He was himself again—powerful young Alexis St. Martin, one of the Fur Company's best and strongest voyageurs.

"St. Martin!" a voice shouted.

"My friend!" Alexis shouted back, pushing his way toward the caller.

But he didn't receive the welcome he'd expected. Instead the man reached for Alexis' shirt and yelled, "Here he is! The man with a lid on his stomach! Now we can see it!"

Alexis hugged his shirt close to his body. "No!" he said, twisting away.

But now more hands were clutching at him, dragging his shirt upward, exposing the scar tissue and the plugged hole in his stomach. And everyone around him was laughing.

"Ah! But the lid is so small!" someone said.

"Pull it out so we can see the hole!" another insisted.

It was a long time before they tired of the sport and finally let him go.

Later, huddled out of sight beyond the glow of the fires, Alexis shook with anger. Then the anger faded and he made himself face the truth. He was not a clever man, but he understood that no matter how well and strong he had become, voyageurs who knew about his injury would always see him as a joke, something to laugh at. His old friends would never again accept him as their equal. To them, he had become a freak—no longer a man, but only the-man-with-a-hole-in-his-stomach.

Dawn was breaking when Alexis started back up the hill toward the fort. By then he was telling himself that the voyageurs working out of Mackinac Island were not the only ones in the world. There were others, those who worked for the fur traders of the Hudson Bay Company of Canada, for example. They would know nothing about Alexis St. Martin if he suddenly appeared among them. They would see only that he had the strength and stamina a voyageur needed. With them, he assured himself, he could once more do the only work he had ever wanted to do.

He didn't know how to get back home to Canada, where he could offer himself to the Hudson Bay Company's hiring agents. He had no money or means of travel. But he had made up his mind to reach those agents, in one way or another, and as soon as possible.

In the meantime he was dependent on Dr. Beaumont for food and shelter. He would have to go on being the doctor's obedient servant until he could become his own man again.

4 / DR. BEAUMONT'S LABORATORY: ALEXIS' STOMACH

Dr. Beaumont's notes said Alexis was now "active, athletic and vigorous; exercising, eating and drinking like other active people." Of course he did still have one remaining sign of that terrible wound. He still had that hole in his stomach, that fistula as the doctor called it when he was using medical terms.

The doctor therefore couldn't write an article claiming that his treatment of Alexis had left him completely healed. But now the doctor scarcely cared about that. The article was no longer as important to him as it had been. He didn't even wish he could close that fistula. He had decided to make use of it instead.

Through that fistula, he believed, he could solve the mystery of digestion which men had been trying to solve for centuries. And the fame he would win, if he succeeded, would reach far beyond the world of medicine. It would be the kind of fame he'd always dreamed of.

Doctors already knew, in his day, that the process of digestion transformed food into a soft gruel-like substance called chyme, which then moved on out of the stomach into the intestines. But no one yet knew how that process occurred.

Some said the stomach grew warm enough to "cook" the food until it was softened into chyme.

Others said that the walls of the stomach moved in such a way that they ground food up, almost as if the food were in a grinding mill.

Dr. Beaumont himself, and most medical men of his time, had still another idea. They believed food was dissolved into chyme by the action of a liquid they called gastric juice. But they didn't know what gastric juice was or exactly what—if anything—it did.

It had now occurred to Dr. Beaumont that he, of all the doctors in the world, could perform experiments that would learn the truth.

The doctor didn't consult Alexis about those experiments, of course, but he wanted the Surgeon-General's approval of his plan. He wrote to ask for it, and sent along his article called simply "A Case of Wounded Stomach."

Dr. Lovell liked the idea that one of his army doctors might do some important research. He encouraged Dr. Beaumont to go ahead. He also said his "highly creditable" article would be published within a few months, in January 1825, in the important *Medical Recorder.*

Dr. Beaumont wrote Dr. Lovell once more. He wanted to

leave Mackinac Island, he said. If he did his experiments there, where he was the only doctor for hundreds of miles, they might be questioned. He might even be accused of inventing his remarkable case. In some eastern town, on the other hand, he could show Alexis' fistula to doctors who could then guarantee its existence.

Dr. Lovell arranged a transfer. In the spring of 1825 Dr. Beaumont took Alexis and his family to his new post at Fort Niagara in New York State. There, on the first of August, he was ready to begin his experiments.

First he set out small bits of seven kinds of food: cooked beef that he called à la mode beef, raw salted beef, boiled salted beef, fat pork, stale bread, and shredded cabbage. Then he tied each of them, one after the other, on a length of silk string.

Finally he called Alexis. "Take off your shirt and lie down," he ordered.

Alexis had often done that to have his wound dressed. He obeyed.

Dr. Beaumont removed the plug of lint and thrust his silk string with its row of bits of food through the hole. He left the end of the string outside and plugged the hole up again.

"You can finish bringing in the wood now," he told Alexis. He looked at his watch to check the time. It was exactly noon.

He made neat notes that day about the foods in Alexis' stomach:

> At 1 o'clock, P.M., withdrew and examined them—found the *cabbage* and *bread* about half digested; the pieces of *meat* unchanged. Returned them to the stomach.
>
> At 2 o'clock, P.M., withdrew them again—found the *cabbage, pork,* and *boiled beef,* all cleanly digested, and gone from the string; the other pieces of meat but very little affected. Returned them to the stomach again.

The doctor was delighted. Already he had learned that the stomach did not digest all of one kind of food first, "then all of the second, and so on," as Dr. Lovell had suggested might be so. It didn't digest all foods at the same rate, but it did digest several at the same time.

At 3 o'clock he checked once more. Now the à la mode beef was partly digested. The raw beef had changed only on its surface.

Alexis was finding the whole business painful. He told the doctor his stomach hurt.

The doctor examined his subject's stomach. It appeared normal to him, and that was all Dr. Beaumont cared about. He put the remaining foods back into it.

At 4 o'clock, when he withdrew them again, Alexis said the pain in his stomach was worse. He also said his head ached and that he felt very weak. And this time the doctor decided the condition of the stomach was no longer right for his experiment.

Alexis didn't recover for a week. The doctor was in a fury of impatience by the time he was finally able to start experimenting again on August 7.

That day he put a thermometer into Alexis' stomach and found it registered 100 degrees, only two degrees above that of a healthy person's mouth.

"So the stomach is not hot enough to 'cook' food," he concluded.

Next he wanted to study the affect of gastric juice, that clear liquid that accumulated inside the stomach. If it digested food by dissolving it, as so many believed, then it should be able to dissolve food outside the stomach as well as inside it. With a rubber tube, he withdrew an ounce of the juice and put it in a vial which he kept at stomach-temperature in warm water.

Then he got two small pieces of boiled salted beef and put one of them in the vial and the other in Alexis' stomach. He checked both regularly.

The surface of the meat in the stomach quickly became loose and started to fall away. Within two hours, by 1 o'clock that afternoon, the meat was "all completely digested and gone."

The meat in the vial was disappearing too, but more slowly. Dr. Beaumont shook the vial, after a time, to imitate what he called the "motion" of the stomach. By 9 o'clock that meat too was "completely digested."

No doubt the shaking had helped, he thought. Nevertheless he was now convinced that the process of digestion was brought about almost entirely by the action of the gastric juice.

He felt he was making important discoveries. He was eager to let others know about them. During the furlough that was now due him, he planned to meet with doctors in several eastern cities, tell them about his experiments, and show them his subject's fistula.

He knew, of course, that Alexis would probably raise a fuss when he was told to stand, naked from the waist up, in front of strangers.

"He is completely ignorant of science," Dr. Beaumont told a fellow officer. "He seems to think that fascinating fistula of his is something shameful, to be hidden. But he knows I expect obedience," he added confidently. "He'll do as I tell him."

The first stop on their trip was Plattsburgh, where Deborah and her children had been visiting her family. The morning after they arrived, the doctor called out for Alexis. There was no answer. He called again. Finally Dr. Beaumont went in search of his subject, but he was not to be found.

Someone had told the former voyageur that the Canadian border was only a few miles away to the north, and that Montreal—and therefore his own village—lay scarcely two days walk beyond.

Alexis' chance had come at last. He had waited only until the household was asleep, and then he had crept out into the night. He headed north by the stars. By morning, when the doctor was searching for him, he was safely back in his own country and on his way home.

5 / MORE EXPERIMENTS

Dr. Beaumont found it hard to believe that the "ungrateful wretch," as he called Alexis, was actually gone. But as soon as he accepted the fact, he made up his mind to get his subject back. He assumed Alexis had returned to his Canadian homeland, so he asked the Fur Company's hiring agents for help. They were to keep a sharp eye out for the-man-with-the-hole-in-his-stomach and return him to the doctor if they found him.

Alexis, in the meantime, was doing just what he'd hoped to do. First he'd courted young Marie Jolly, a French-Canadian like himself. And after they were married he signed on as a voyageur with the Hudson Bay Company.

Two years went by. Dr. Beaumont was stationed once again in the Michigan Territory at Fort Howard. He and his family lived through an Indian uprising there. But even that didn't put his experiments out of his mind for long. Finally, in the summer of 1827, he had a letter from a Fur Company agent. Alexis had been found!

By then Alexis had learned the sad truth. He was no longer fit to be a voyageur. His wound and his years as an invalid had left him unable to paddle the bateau tirelessly for days. He couldn't carry a voyageur's heavy loads overland. Now he was chopping wood and doing other odd jobs to support Marie and their baby.

The agent who found him wrote that Alexis was "poor and miserable beyond description." But, he added, "He is *Married*" and would not leave his wife.

Dr. Beaumont urged the agent to talk to Alexis again and convince him to change his mind.

The mails were slow. Weeks passed. Then came a letter saying that Alexis St. Martin now seemed willing to return for a year or two "for a reasonable wage" and "providing you will employ his Wife!!!" In a final sentence the agent added that Alexis now had another offer of support from a doctor in Montreal.

"So!" Dr. Beaumont roared when he read that last line. "My patient is willing to help a strange doctor become famous by performing experiments on him! Am I not the one who saved his life, who supported him for years?"

"But Alexis has said he will come to thee," Deborah reminded him.

"But only if I pay him cash! Room and board are no longer enough for him!" Dr. Beaumont shook the letter he was holding. "And he wants his wife to be paid as well!"

42 /

"I would be glad of a woman's help," Deborah said quietly. She now had a second two-year-old daughter and a newborn son.

"Any wife of Alexis' would doubtless be more trouble to you than use," the doctor muttered. But he knew he was going to accept the terms Alexis had set. If he did anything else, the Montreal doctor would probably win the fame that only he, Dr. Beaumont, was entitled to.

In August 1829 a fur company bateau brought Alexis and Marie to the doctor's new post at Fort Crawford on the upper Mississippi. The bateau also brought the St. Martin's two children.

"He is an even worse scoundrel than I thought!" Dr. Beaumont told Deborah. "Now he saddles me with his whole family."

But now that his subject was back, after four long years, the doctor was eager to get on with his work. He made a list of questions and planned the experiments he hoped would answer them.

One question was: Is there always gastric juice in the stomach, or does it flow out of the small cells in the stomach wall only when food is present?

To answer that question, Dr. Beaumont made Alexis go without food for many hours. When his stomach was completely empty, the doctor said, "Lie down beside the window, on your side. No—this way! Don't move."

A beam of sunlight was shining straight through the fistula. Dr. Beaumont, peering into Alexis' stomach through a magnifying glass, could see no juice in the cavity. And when he pushed a rubber tube into the stomach, he could not draw any juice up into the tube.

"Now I shall find out what will cause the juice to flow," he said.

He dropped a few crumbs of bread into the stomach. Soon they became moist. At the same time Dr. Beaumont was able to draw juice up through his tube.

For another experiment he prodded the wall of Alexis' empty stomach with the end of the tube. For some fifteen minutes he continued this "irritation," as he called it. At the end of that time he was able to draw up more than an ounce of juice.

He repeated these experiments time after time. Finally he wrote that both food and any "irritating substance" set off the action of "the gastric vessels."

Whenever the doctor wasn't using him in an experiment, Alexis was kept busy. He was still carrying out "all the duties of a common servant," as Dr. Beaumont put it.

"You do too much," Marie often told her husband. Sometimes she marched into the room where the doctor was "irritating" Alexis' stomach.

"Alexis must come with me now," she said firmly. "You told him he could eat no breakfast, so now he must have his dinner."

"I knew that woman would be of more trouble than use," the doctor often grumbled to Deborah.

Another question on his list was this: Which foods digest

most rapidly in the stomach? To answer it the doctor regularly examined the contents of Alexis' stomach after meals. Finally he was able to make out a chart showing that roast pork, for example, took 5¼ hours to digest, and that roast beef and sour apples and cake each took 3 hours. Boiled rice, his chart showed, digested in a single hour.

Dr. Beaumont also discovered that food digests most rapidly if it enters the stomach in very small pieces—if, for example, it has been thoroughly chewed before it is swallowed.

One morning, as Alexis ate his breakfast of fat pork, bread and potatoes, he was still angry over the doctor's rudeness to Marie the day before. Four hours later the doctor found that the food Alexis had eaten was still in his stomach. It was undigested and mixed with bile. Bile, a bitter yellow fluid which comes from the liver, is not usually found in the stomach.

"It seems clear," Dr. Beaumont told Deborah that evening, "that anger produces bile, and that bile prevents good digestion."

"That is a most important discovery!" Deborah said. She was pleased that her husband was doing work that might earn him the fame he craved. Then she smiled and added, "The next time thee is angry, I will remember not to give thee any dinner until thy temper has cooled."

There was one question on Dr. Beaumont's list which he knew he could never answer. It was: What is gastric juice?

He had touched his finger to the juice taken from Alexis' stomach, and tasted it. He was sure it was some kind of acid.

Other men too had said that gastric juice was probably an acid—perhaps hydrochloric acid, some said. But no one really knew. And Dr. Beaumont realized that only a trained chemist might be able to analyze the liquid and find out what it was.

The expert chemists of that day, however—like the expert scientists in most fields—lived in Europe. And they had no supply of gastric juice to study. So Dr. Beaumont asked for a year's furlough. He planned to take Alexis to Europe and give samples of his gastric juice to any chemist who would analyze it.

When he was sure the furlough would be granted, he began to make plans. First he wanted to get rid of that troublesome woman, Marie. He knew she had been growing homesick, so he told her and Alexis, "I will send you and your children all home to Canada.

"You and the children will remain there, Marie," he went on. "But you, Alexis, will return to me in six months."

"He will not come alone!" Marie said.

"He will," Dr. Beaumont assured her, "because I shall take him to Paris."

The look in Alexis' eyes told him he had offered the one bait no French-Canadian could refuse.

"Paris!" Alexis said, Then he embraced Marie. "I can tell you of all its wonders when I return," he said. "And think how proud our children will be when they can say their father has seen Paris!"

6 / A FAMOUS BOOK, TWO FAMOUS MEN

While the St. Martin family went north to Canada, the doctor and his own family visited in Plattsburgh. Deborah would stay there, with her children, while her husband was away.

At the end of six months Alexis reappeared. The doctor had been sure he would. But to make certain that he would have no future worry about Alexis, Dr. Beaumont had prepared a contract which he read aloud to him. It said Alexis would serve the doctor "faithfully" and submit to any experiments he might wish to make "on or in the stomach of him." In return Alexis would receive food, lodging and clothes for one year, and $150, a large sum of money for a French-Canadian villager.

"Put your X on this line," Dr. Beaumont told Alexis.

Alexis did as he was told.

Then Dr. Beaumont took him to Washington. But they didn't go on to Europe.

"My furlough has been cut to six months," the doctor said. "It's not worth going abroad for such a short time. We shall remain here instead."

Alexis was stunned. He wasn't going to see Paris after all!

He was so upset that Dr. Beaumont was afraid he might run off again in spite of their signed contract. So with Dr. Lovell's help he had his subject enlisted in the army, as a sergeant. And he warned Alexis that deserters from the army were always caught and thrown into prison.

Alexis was angry and bitter. He missed his wife and children. The only way he could forget his troubles was to get drunk. Always, as soon as he was sober again, he had to face a terrible tongue-lashing from the doctor. But he could stand even the doctor's rage better than he could endure his lonely misery.

Dr. Beaumont, on the other hand, was enjoying the busy capital after his years in the wilderness. He exhibited Alexis to any doctor who was interested. He read medical textbooks he had never had a chance to read at his army posts.

In those books he learned that an Italian scientist, Lazzaro Spallanzani, had obtained some of his own gastric juice by making himself vomit. Spallanzani had reported that the juice would digest food even outside the stomach. But he had never been able to obtain enough of his gastric juice to perform all the experiments he wished.

Most of the scientists Dr. Beaumont read about, however, had not even tried to experiment. They had not had the

advantage of a live human subject to work with. But that had not prevented them from using their imaginations to invent theories about digestion, and announcing those theories with great authority. Dr. Beaumont, who now thought many of those theories were mistaken, believed that through his own experiments he was finally learning the truth about what happened inside a human stomach.

One thing his books didn't tell him was an answer to that question: What is gastric juice? So he sent a bottle of the fluid from Alexis' stomach to a famous Swedish chemist and waited impatiently for a response.

He had been meeting many important people in Washington. They treated him as if he were important too. They even suggested that he do just what he'd secretly been planning to do. They suggested that he write a book about his experiments on Alexis. He started it immediately.

When his furlough in Washington was over, he was made recruiting officer in Plattsburgh. That job gave him free time for his new task and the help of his doctor cousin, Samuel Beaumont. He had found, as he said, that it was proving "an immense job to make a *Book*."

Dr. Beaumont allowed Alexis to leave Plattsburgh long enough for a trip home. He was sure the new sergeant would return, out of fear of being tracked down as a deserter. And Alexis did. The book was almost finished by then, and Dr. Beaumont began again "putting in and taking out those little bags of food," as he wrote Dr. Lovell. He had decided to do one more series of experiments while he waited for a report from the famous chemist in Sweden.

But no word came from Sweden. And finally Dr. Beaumont had to publish the book for which he had already taken orders, at $2 a copy. He hoped to make a profit as well as a reputation out of it. It appeared in December 1833, eleven years after that gun blast in the Fur Company store. Its title was *Experiments and Observations on the Gastric Juice and the Physiology of Digestion.*

It was an immediate success. Medical journals praised it to doctors. Newspapers and magazines praised it to the general public. A German publisher had it translated and printed in Germany. Later it was published in other European countries too.

Until then most European scientists had believed that Americans were not able to do any serious work in the field of science. Now they had to admit that Dr. Beaumont's book proved they were wrong.

Suddenly doctors everywhere wanted to see Dr. Beaumont and his remarkable case. Alexis was put on exhibition in Boston, at a Connecticut Medical Convention, and before classes of students at the Columbian Medical College in Washington.

Then word reached the doctor that the American ambassador to France wanted him to bring the-man-with-the-hole-in-his-stomach to Paris. Dr. Beaumont, more delighted every day with his growing reputation, told Alexis he could visit his family before they left for Europe.

Alexis went home. Dr. Beaumont was confident he would once more return in good time.

But Alexis felt he had been fooled once by the promise of a trip to Paris. He wasn't going to be fooled again. And perhaps someone had told him that a deserter from the American army would be safe if he stayed in Canada. He asked his village priest to write a letter for him, a letter to Dr. Beaumont.

"Dear Sir," it began, "My wife is not willing for me to go, for she thinks I can do a great deal better to stay at home . . . "

A furious Dr. Beaumont wrote to Alexis ordering him to come back. There was no answer to that letter or to others he sent. When he had to leave Plattsburgh for a new post near St. Louis, Missouri, he told his cousin to continue the letter-writing. He also sought help from the American Fur Company traders.

Finally Dr. Beaumont did get a letter, perhaps written for Alexis by a doctor. It said that a medical society in Boston wished to engage Alexis "for the purpose of experiments," but that he would not accept the offer "without your approbation and consent."

"Should you desire me to join you with my family," the letter added, "I am ready at any time."

Alexis was being stubborn, refusing to come without his family. Dr. Beaumont was just as stubborn, refusing to burden himself with Marie and the children again. He did offer Alexis money for his family's support if Alexis would come to him by himself. Alexis still refused.

The two men sent letters back and forth for years, even after the doctor had retired from the army and grown prosperous on his private medical practice in St. Louis. Dr. Beaumont wrote his last letter to Alexis shortly before his own death on April 25, 1853, at the age of sixty-eight.

The doctor had become every bit as famous as he'd hoped to be. He was honored all over the world during his last years. One scientist who praised him, the German Theodor Schwann, also carried forward his work. In 1836 Schwann analyzed gastric juice and found that it did indeed contain hydrochloric acid along with another substance called pepsin.

But Dr. Beaumont himself had learned almost as much about the process of digestion as is known to this day. And he had opened the way to the new science of nutrition, the study of food and how the body makes use of it.

Alexis St. Martin didn't die until 1880, at the age of eighty-three. He had outlived the doctor by twenty-seven years. During those years he was invited to appear before many medical societies and other interested groups. Since he too had become famous, he was treated with great courtesy and offered generous fees.

Alexis accepted a good many of those invitations. His fees helped support the family that crowded his little house—four married children and a flock of grandchildren. Perhaps, too, he had grown so used to being stared at that he no longer minded it so much. Or maybe, by then, he was even proud to stand in public, naked to the waist, and let people see that hole in his stomach through which the world had gained so much valuable new knowledge.

SELECTED BIBLIOGRAPHY

The Beaumont Papers (letters, notebooks, clippings, etc.). Library, Washington University School of Medicine, St. Louis.

Bayley, J. R. "Beaumont: Army Surgeon," *Physician & Surgeon*, 1900.

Broadman, Estelle. "Relationship between Joseph Lovell and William Beaumont," *Bulletin of the History of Medicine*, March–April 1964.

Broadman, Estelle. "William Beaumont as a Physician," *Wisconsin Medical Journal*, June 1967.

Bylebyl, Jerome J. "William Beaumont, Robley Dunglison and the 'Philadelphia Physicologists,' " *Journal of the History of Medicine and Allied Sciences*, January 1970.

Corbus, B. R. "William Beaumont and His Work in the Light of Modern Research," *Journal Michigan Medical Society*, 1909, V. 8.

Friedenwald, J. and Morrison, S. "Importance of Beaumont's Contribution to Gastro-enterology," *Bulletin of the School of Medicine*, University of Maryland, 1934, V. 18.

Ingelfinger, Franz J. "Gastric Function," *Nutrition Today*, September–October 1971.

Osler, William. "William Beaumont: A Pioneer American Physiologist," *Journal American Medical Association*, 1902, V. 39.

Beaumont, William. *Experiments and Observations on the Gastric Juice and the Physiology of Digestion.* Plattsburgh, New York, 1833 (Facsimile edition 1929 with biographical essay by Sir William Osler; reprinted 1941).

Flexner, James Thomas. *Doctors on Horseback: Pioneers of American Medicine.* New York, 1937.

Haggard, Howard W. *The Doctor in History.* New Haven, 1934.

Myer, J. S. *Life and Letters of Dr. William Beaumont,* with an introduction by Sir William Osler. St. Louis, 1939.

Packard, Francis. *History of Medicine in the United States.* New York, 1931.

Widder, Keith R. *Reveille Till Taps: Soldier Life at Fort Mackinac 1780–1895* Mackinac Island, 1972.

Jewett, C. Harvey. "William Beaumont," speech to Malcolm S. Woodbury Historical Society, January 26, 1935.

Patterson, Robert U. "William Beaumont as an Army Officer," speech to New York Academy of Medicine, October 5, 1953.

Schlueter, Robert E. "A short biographical sketch of Dr. William Beaumont (1785–1853)," speech to medical staff and resident Sisters at St. Anthony's Hospital, St. Louis, December 9, 1935.

ABOUT THE AUTHORS

Sam and Beryl Epstein have written both adult and juvenile books. The titles range over a wide variety of subjects. This is their second book for Coward, McCann & Geoghegan's Science Discovery series. Their first, *Mister Peale's Mammoth*, about the painter Charles Willson Peale's search for the skeleton of a mammoth, was a Junior Literary Guild selection.

The Epsteins live in Southold, New York.

ABOUT THE ARTIST

Joseph Scrofani became a freelance illustrator after graduating from the Parsons School of Design. For Coward, McCann & Geoghegan he has illustrated *Adam and the Wishing Charm*, by Marietta Moskin. His drawings appear frequently on the pages of the New York *Times,* as well as in magazines such as *Natural History* and *Saturday Review*. He lives in Fort Lee, New Jersey.

You can make many more science discoveries.

SCIENCE DISCOVERY BOOKS

MARY'S MONSTER
by Ruth Van Ness Blair/illustrated by Richard Cuffari

"This true story of the discovery of the Ichthyosaurus by 12-year-old Mary Ann Anning in 1811 combines colorful details of life in early 19th century England and interesting facts about fossils and dinosaurs." —*School Library Journal*

"A compelling book for young scientists, skillfully illustrated." —*Publishers Weekly*

COILS, MAGNETS, AND RINGS:
Michael Faraday's World
by Nancy Veglahn/illustrated by Christopher Spollen

"Veglahn maintains a high human interest from the very first sentence, without resorting to any extraneous fictionalized episodes but simply by conveying Faraday's own unbounded curiosity and intense absorption in his pursuit of answers."
—*Kirkus Reviews*

". . . non-technical descriptions of Faraday's work including the coils, magnets, and rings experiment in which he discovered electromagnetic induction . . . . Spollen's bold black-and-white drawings, appearing throughout, supply a portrait of the period." —*School Library Journal*

Both chosen as Outstanding Science Trade Books by the National Science Teachers Association/Children's Book Council Joint Committee.

LOOK FOR

THE MYSTERIOUS RAYS:
Marie Curie's World
by Nancy Veglahn/illustrated by Victor Juhasz

DARWIN AND THE ENCHANTED ISLES
by Irwin Shapiro/illustrated by Christopher Spollen